Times Square

Times Square

JANA ASTON

Times Square

Edited by RJ Locksley
Cover Design by Letitia Hasser
Cover Photographer: Lauren Perry
Formatting by Erik Gevers

Dedication

For Lauren,
Thank you for messaging me during your Starbucks
adventures.

One

Once in a while, right in the middle of an ordinary life, love gives us a fairy tale.

I saw that quote about fairy tales stamped on a decorative canvas at a home decorating store. I didn't buy it because I don't have a home to put it in. Also because I don't believe in fairy tales. Honestly, it pisses me off. Retail propaganda aims to promote love. Don't believe me? I couldn't find a single decorative sign that said, *Once in a while, right after you move in with your fiancé, you realize he's sleeping with someone else.*

Nope. Not a one. Granted, that's sorta specific, but it's not like I could find one that said *You Don't Need Him or Keep Your Pants On, Asshole* either. And seeing how the Home Stop had four aisles dedicated to wedding crap and zero to alcohol, I think their agenda was clear.

That's fine. Because my agenda is clear too.

Get promoted.

Get my own apartment, or at least my own bedroom.

Do not get distracted by a pretty face with a big dick.

These are all more difficult than you'd expect and I'll give you three reasons why.

New.

York.

City.

I grew up on *Sex and the City* too. I get it. New York seems romantic and full of promise. The Big Apple. The city that never sleeps. The place that dreams are made of. If you can make it here, you can make it anywhere.

It's the only city in the world where you can buy a cupcake from a vending machine, get Pad Thai delivered at three AM and do your laundry in a twenty-four-hour laundromat with organic detergent and free wifi.

The wardrobes are to kill for and shoes that cost more than the average American's monthly mortgage payment are regularly paraded down the same sidewalks dogs piss on.

What you don't anticipate is paying seven hundred dollars a month to share a one-bedroom apartment with three other girls. Bunk beds, in case you're wondering.

Or a job in marketing that is so entry-level that my duties don't amount to much more than data entry.

Or the knowledge that you can't afford the amazing middle-of-the-night food delivery and even those vending machine cupcakes need to be budgeted into your monthly food expenses.

That's why I came to New York in the first place, because the possibilities are endless here. Actually, that's a lie. I came to New York because my fiancé was here. My ex, Brad. He's still here, he's just no longer my fiancé. He graduated a year before I did and got a job in New York City. The plan was that I'd follow him when I graduated, which I did.

I didn't realize the plan included him sleeping with other women while he waited.

In our apartment, no less. An apartment I'd helped him move into while he'd talked about how great the space would be for both of us. It was a great apartment. I

2

really enjoyed it for the few weeks I lived there. For the few weeks I still thought we had a future together.

Looking back, I'm not sure how I didn't see it sooner.

Looking back, it should have been so clear, but clearly my hunches are shit. He'd been so eager for me to move to New York. Talking about the things we'd do once I got here, saving me closet space so he wouldn't get used to using it before I moved in. Just six months before I moved—when he'd been home for Christmas—he'd mentioned how the following year he'd be taking me to see the Christmas tree in Rockefeller Center.

We didn't make it to the following year. We didn't even make it through the summer before I realized I should have listened to my gut. Before I realized that the pair of panties I found in his apartment were not a mistake made by his laundry service. Before I realized there was no need for him to excuse himself for incoming calls from numbers labeled 'Brady' or 'Chip,' unless they were really 'Brandys' or 'Christines.'

My bad.

When I packed two suitcases and got on a direct flight to LaGuardia a year ago I thought I knew where my life was headed. The fact that I was moving with two suitcases by myself after helping Brad drive his stuff across four states should have been my first clue that I thought wrong. But it's okay because New York is also a place of fresh starts, of renewal and rebirth, and my story isn't over yet. Not even close.

Also, I know two suitcases sounds meager, but I mentioned the roommate situation, right? Top-bunk girls share a dresser, bottom-bunk girls get the space under the beds. Packing light turned out to be an accurate forecast of my future.

I really, really need to move.

Don't get me wrong, it's a nice place. A West Village-address elevator building. It's not bad, just crowded. Though to be fair, one of the girls is a flight attendant and sometimes we don't see her for a couple of days at a time, which is a huge bonus on bathroom time.

But still.

I've got goals. I graduated from Iowa. University of, not State. Go Hawkeyes. I know I have to work my way up the corporate ladder and I can. I will. I have to. Mainly because student loans are no joke and I don't want to go back to Iowa. Because New York City, for all its flaws, really is kind of magical. Limitless. The energy is a tangible vibe that you feel every day, a jolt more effective than any caffeine.

So moving on and all that. I found the apartment in New York through an old college friend—she's one of the roommates. She's a perfect size four. Apparently some women are a size four, but not perfectly. I don't get it either, but it means she gets paid a hundred dollars an hour to be a fit model. Only in New York, right? It's a great gig—when you can get it. Turns out most fit models don't work forty hours a week—my roommate only books six to eight hours a week, so she has to supplement it with waitressing.

I found the job through our other roommate. She was dating a guy who worked in the IT department and told me there were openings in marketing. I got the job and he got a five-hundred-dollar referral bonus. Two weeks later he gave my roommate chlamydia and they broke up. It's exactly as awkward as you'd imagine it is when I see him at work, which thankfully isn't often.

I was offered two jobs that week, but I had a really good feeling about this one, so I went with my gut.

I ended up placed with a supervisor who is a total

nightmare. Yay for my amazing intuition.

But it's a good company. There's a lot of room for advancement and I'll need a promotion or two if I'm ever going to get my own place.

Which is why I cannot be distracted by the hot guy I just caught staring at me from across Starbucks.

Sometimes I stop here on my way home from work. I splurge on a plain black coffee and use their free wifi and enjoy the peace and quiet while I blog. I know technically a Starbucks in Manhattan isn't that peaceful or that quiet, but unlike my apartment no one here will try to talk to me.

He's spinning his phone in his hand and making no attempt not to be caught staring at me. I smile in a polite *I can see you staring at me* kind of way and he drops his phone into his lap. His crotch more specifically. And—I look. Of course I look. And then I catch myself looking and I burst out laughing which must be really loud because three people turn to look at me. You know how headphones kind of mute your own noise? Oops.

He really is attractive. And in New York models are everywhere. He looks like he falls into that category: under thirty, fit, attractive and cocky. Literally. And he looks like a guy I'd see on a billboard for men's cologne or something.

A willowy female slides into the empty seat across from him and starts talking a mile a minute. She looks like a model as well. Tall, thin, gorgeous and dressed like she just came from a go-see. Her dark hair is pulled into a low ponytail and her delicate fingers are polish-free as she waves them around while she speaks. He breaks his gaze from mine for a moment to greet her before flicking his eyes back my way.

I laugh again, a little shocked that he's ignoring the

beautiful creature before him to partake in whatever weird flirting he thinks he's doing with me. He's full-on smiling now—at me—while the girl continues to chatter away.

I raise an eyebrow at him in disbelief.

He raises his in return.

I just shake my head and blush.

This guy is like four levels of hotter than I'm used to dealing with. The girl finally turns to see what's got him so distracted and she smiles at me.

Oh, hell, no—I bet they're one of those kinky couples looking for a unicorn. You know, a single girl willing to join an existing couple for a threesome? I'm not into that no matter how hot he is. Firm no. I turn my attention back to my laptop and the blog post I'm working on. *Ignore him,* I tell myself. *Focus on what you came here for.*

What I came here for is some peace and quiet so I can finish this review for my book blog. Then it hits me. The book I just finished was about a threesome, and I loved it. I burst out laughing all over again. Oh, the ridiculous irony. But hey, just because I like to read about something doesn't mean I want to *do* it.

When I look back up the girl is gone and he's still there. This time he raises an eyebrow at me and then stands—and heads in my direction.

I drop my eyes to my screen and realize I was in the middle of making a graphic for the review. A really racy graphic with three semi-dressed people. Oh, fuck, abort! I snap the lid of my laptop closed half a second before he stops at my table.

"I couldn't help but notice you," he says by way of hello.

I bet, I think.

"It's nice to see a beautiful woman not afraid to

laugh," he continues and it catches me by surprise. This isn't where I thought the conversation was headed.

"Thank you?" I say, but it comes out more like a question than an affirmation.

"You're welcome," he replies. "But you shouldn't sound so uneasy when you receive a compliment."

I blink, a little unsure how to take him.

"What's your name?"

"Lauren," I find myself telling him, but I'm not sure why. My go-to name for creepers is Samantha. Why did I give him my real name?

"Lauren," he repeats with a nod. "Would you mind if I asked you a question?"

"Um, okay," I reply. Oh, shit. He's going to invite me to a three-way now. I'm so not ready. "Wait," I blurt out.

"Wait?" He smiles at me, and damned if he doesn't have the cutest dimples ever. Dimples are supposedly a genetic deformity and I find myself wondering if it hurts his modeling. Probably not because it's somehow adorable and erotic simultaneously. He probably gets paid extra for them. I wonder if they're insured.

"Well, first you should tell me your name too." Ugh. That's the best line I can come up with? Lame.

"Max," he replies with a small tilt of his head and a bemused expression on his face.

"Okay." I nod. And because I really have no game I shrug and blurt, "What?"

"What were you looking at online that had you so entranced?"

"Oh." I glance down at my closed laptop and back to him. "I'm a blogger. I was working on a book review." He nods and I notice his hair is slightly damp, as if he just came from the gym. It's dark and his eyes are the most seductive shade of blue. I'm still not doing the threesome.

Nope, no way.

"What kind of books do you read?"

"Smut mostly," I blurt out before I think better of it. I feel my face heat up while he smirks.

"Nothing wrong with reading a little smut, Lauren. But it's even better to act it out."

Holy. Hell.

Then he winks at me, turns around and walks out.

Only in New York, right? And holy crap, now I'm all hot and bothered and I can't even go home and masturbate because the apartment is always occupied. Always! And I've never successfully been able to get myself off in the shower, dammit to hell.

I tightly cross my legs while opening my laptop again. I really need my own place.

Two

I wake up the next morning before my alarm—as per usual. Someone is always creeping in and out of the bedroom in the mornings. Luckily the bathroom in this apartment is off the living room, so that cuts down on the noise a little. We also keep a vanity table set up in place of a kitchen table to create a hair-and-makeup zone, keeping the bathroom open as much as possible.

But someone is in the bathroom now, so I'll have to wait. No biggie. I plan my morning routine around this, so when my alarm sounds I hit the snooze button and stretch out under the covers to wait.

In retrospect, that's the exact moment when this day goes to shit.

Because somehow, inconceivably, in an apartment shared with three other girls, I wake up an hour later to complete silence. And now I'm late. Really late.

"No, no, no, no, no!" I mutter while tossing the covers off and dropping out of bed. I drop because I'm a top-bunker and I don't have time to use the ladder and oh, holy shit, how does my life include a ladder required to get in and out of bed?

My feet hit the floor, but one lands on a sock and my foot skids until my pinky toe bangs into the milk crate my bottom bunkmate has been using as a nightstand. I do that weird dropped-open-mouth thing one does when they hurt themselves right before they swear, which I do next. How? How did I even just do that? I hop around for a second while I do the math on how I'm going to make it to work on time. Then I bolt for the shower and thank the water gods that it's hot before jumping in.

I'm out in under a minute, sans hair wash. No time. I'll spray some dry shampoo on and make the best of it. I've got a perfect record at work. I'm always on time, always dependable, and I don't need today to ruin that. Especially when I'm applying for promotions.

Plus my boss is a bitch of the worst degree. I'm pretty sure she hates me so I'm not going to give her anything to use against me. No way, no how. I just have to pay my dues and then get promoted out of her department. Fingers crossed.

Teeth brushed, pants on, blouse buttoned and I'm flying out the door. And… the elevator has two strips of yellow caution tape forming an x across the doors. *Okay, Lauren. Just breathe, you got this. Six flights is not that many.* I shove open the stairwell door and keep one hand on the rail as I book it down the stairs as fast as my feet will move, my sneakers thumping on the concrete steps and echoing through the stairwell. I don't have time to care about the racket I'm making, I'm just counting my blessings that it's only six flights.

Shoving open the door on the ground level, I sling my purse across my body and make a run for the subway. I think I've still got this, as long as the trains are running on time I'm going to make it with a few minutes to spare.

I'm two minutes into my run when I remember I forgot to grab my office shoes on the way out the door. Dammit, I hope I have a pair of flats in my drawer at the office or I'm going to be stuck in these all day and my boss will make a snide comment about millennial shoe choices while pretending it's a joke.

No, it won't be a joke. And yes, she will be wearing shoes that cost more than my rent. But I'm so going to make it on time, so she can suck it! I sigh in relief as I run down the stairs into the Fourteenth Street Station and squeeze through the turnstiles in time to make my train. Once on, I score a seat and get to work. First I pull a brush out of my bag and get to work taming my blonde hair into a perfect ponytail with lots of volume and a final strand of hair wrapped around the band and fastened with a bobby pin to cover the elastic. I watched a video online once and now I can do it without a mirror and in motion when necessary.

My makeup is done via a compact mirror and finished before I reach my stop. Then I walk another five blocks to my office. In Manhattan it's called walking but anywhere else that pace would be considered a jog. I check my phone when I'm a block away—the building is in my sights—and grin. I made it.

I've even got just enough time to grab a coffee from the little shop located next door to my building, as long as they don't have a line. They only charge a dollar for a coffee to go, which even I can afford, and when I approach the door and see no line I'm tempted to click my sneaker-clad heels together. No line! I'm still getting my morning coffee! Which really makes all the difference, you know? When I don't have time to stop or the line is too long it throws off my whole morning. I need that cup like a baby needs a pacifier. It's like a cup of zen to get me through my morning, no matter what the boss throws at me.

See, today is totally my day because life is all what you

make of it. I could be pissed off about oversleeping, but no. I'm going to call that sleeping in and still making it to work on time. *A total win, yay me,* I think as I double-check the time and reach for the door handle of the coffee shop.

The door doesn't budge because it's locked. My brain registers this at the same time it registers the orange eight-by-ten sticker stuck to the door. The one labeled New York City Health Department with a big check mark next to 'closed for health code violations' which cannot be possible because I just got coffee here yesterday. And the day before that. And the day before that.

Wait.

Oh, shit. I get coffee here every day.

At the place closed for health code violations. Well, that's great.

Walking next door, I swipe my badge to get past security while wondering if coffee can be contaminated. It can, right? Like bacteria in the machines or something? Never mind, I'm fine. My stomach is okay. I think. I might need to talk myself out of phantom hypochondriac stomach issues, but I'm probably fine.

I need a refund on this day and it's not even nine AM.

I sigh before giving myself a pep talk. *It's fine, Lauren. This day can only get better. Nowhere to go but up, blah blah.* I work in marketing, so I know it's all in how I spin it and I've already determined that today is a good day for a good day, so it will be. I'm going to have a good day if it fucking kills me.

Three

It might just kill me.

"You want me to do what?" I glance across my boss's desk in shock. Surely I am misunderstanding something because there is no possible way I am hearing this correctly.

"I want you to go down to Times Square and pass out some flyers, Lauren. Was that unclear?"

I hate the way she says my name. I don't even like hearing my name come out of her mouth, but the tone she says it in makes it all the worse. And she's always adding it to sentences needlessly to intimidate me. Normal people don't repeat your name to you in conversation because it's unnecessary.

"Did you have a late night? You seem a little off your game today, Lauren. Has the weekend started early for you?"

See what I mean?

She smiles when she says it but she doesn't mean it. Because she's a bitch. That's really all there is to that.

"No, my weekend hasn't started early. I'm just a little confused about why tourists in Times Square would be interested in a sale at the Budget Bridal Stop in Brooklyn. But I have some ideas about how we could better reach the target audience," I start, but that's as far as I get because she cuts me off.

"I didn't ask for your thoughts, Lauren. If you're interested in a career here you need to learn how to follow direction. The team can only have one leader and that's me."

Sometimes I wonder if she was a bitchy baby. I think she probably was.

"Now I understand this probably isn't the most challenging task you've been given and I can see you're not excited about it, but it needs to be done and I hope I can trust you to handle it like a professional."

I swallow the words 'fuck you,' and place a fake smile on my face as I stand.

"You'll need to change here and then have the car service drop you off in Times Square. The case of flyers is much too heavy to walk with." She adds a big smile that anyone else would think was genuine but I know better.

"Sure thing," I call out as I slide the garment bag off the top of her office door and fold it over my arm as I prepare to leave her office.

"And this shouldn't take more than two hours, Lauren. Please don't waste the entire day on this, okay?"

I bite my lip and nod as I walk out of her office. I stop at my desk to arrange the car service the company uses for a pick-up and then head into the women's bathroom to change.

And that is the story of how I end up in Times Square in a wedding dress.

Fuck. My. Life.

This day is shit. Complete and utter shit and I'm done trying to spin it. Done! It's a good day for nothing is what it is. You know that old saying? It's not you, it's me? It's not me. This day sucks.

Oh, God, this was probably a sample dress. It's likely been tried on a hundred times already and now I'm wearing it and sweating in it and—gross.

I have to swallow the lump in my throat to keep from crying. When I left the office in a wedding dress I almost died. I know it's New York and people should be used to seeing anything and everything, but that doesn't help when it's you. And a woman walking through an office building lobby in a wedding gown is going to get some odd stares.

Walking around Times Square midday on a Friday in a stupid white dress isn't much better.

It's not anything I would have picked out if I'd gotten that far in my wedding planning before booting the fiancé. My mom and my maid of honor would have gone with me and I'd have tried on something resembling a picture I'd torn out of a magazine. I'd have practiced walking down the aisle and stood up on my tiptoes to get an idea of what the length would look like with heels. I'd have twirled a little to get a sense of how the material would move and what it would feel like brushing against my legs.

It might have been a princess style with three-quarter-length lace sleeves and matching lace detail over the bodice. Or maybe a ball gown with a sweetheart bodice. Possibly an A-line with a plunging V-neck and a satin ribbon around the waist. It would not have been this dress. Not this spaghetti-strapped, empire-waisted chiffon dress I'm currently wearing.

I drop the box of flyers at my feet and kick it before grabbing a stack off the top. At least I'm wearing my sneakers. See, everything happens for a reason. These sneakers are like a little gift from the universe right now.

"Huge wedding dress sale!" I call out to a couple of women walking nearby, but they don't even turn their heads. Well, that's a great start. I manage to pass out a couple dozen before I'm asked what my rate is. For the night. Because the guy thinks I'm a hooker.

I tell him to fuck off and contemplate looking for a new job, good company be damned. This is ridiculous.

I'm grabbing another handful of flyers when I'm approached by one of New York's finest. If this ends in me getting arrested I am definitely quitting. I could always move to Hawaii and be a waitress. I've got loads of experience from college. I'd find an outdoor ocean-front restaurant to work at and I'd make more than I do now, plus I'd get to enjoy a million-dollar view and fresh ocean air. Fine, I may have fantasized about this a time or two and done the odd hour or three of research. Visualizing a life of shorts and flip-flops all year long is my escape.

"Miss, you can't perform here. You need to move to one of the blue zones." He points to a section of pavement covered in blue paint.

"What?" I question, glancing over at the area he's pointing at. I'm vaguely familiar with the groups of costume characters and street performers working for tips in Times Square being restricted to designated zones.

"I'm not a street performer," I tell him with a shake of my head. "I'm just telling people about a sale at the Budget Bridal Stop." I hold up a flyer. "See?"

"Solicitations in the blue zone, miss. Move along before I have to ticket you."

Solicitations? I'm not soliciting! Wait, maybe I am. Does advertising a bridal shop sale count as selling? Shit. I pick up my box and walk over to the blue zone while wondering how much a one-way ticket to Honolulu is.

Probably more than I have.

I'm in the blue zone for less than five minutes before some idiot in a superhero costume makes a pass at me. I literally cannot make this shit up.

Twenty minutes after that I get my first tip. A tourist drops a quarter into my box as he walks past. I'm about to yell at him that I'm not a street performer when it hits me.

I left the office without my purse.

Without my phone.

Without my subway card.

Without a return ride.

That's the exact moment I start to cry. I'm not a complete disaster, I don't start sobbing, but my eyes are filling with tears, so I focus on a giant neon sign advertising Broadway's latest hit to try to distract myself from the knowledge that it's a two-and-a-half-mile walk back to the office from Times Square. It's not that I'm incapable of walking that far—it's the idea of walking it in a wedding dress. It's gonna be one hell of a walk of shame, that's for sure.

"Oh, she's doing performance art!"

I blink and focus on the woman standing in front of me. She's clasped her hands together and has a wide smile on her face, staring at me as if she's just discovered a wombat in the middle of the concrete jungle that is the pedestrian plaza in Times Square.

"What are you supposed to be? A jilted bride?"

I start to shake my head but when I do a single tear breaks free and rolls down my cheek. Fuck.

The woman nods and seems satisfied that she's figured me out. "Very well done. Give her a dollar, Frank."

Well then, now I can add performance artist to my resume. Fan-fucking-tastic. I wipe the tear off my cheek and take stock. I've got a dollar twenty-five. I think a single subway ride is three bucks if I remember correctly. It's cheaper to get a MetroCard and buy a monthly pass so that's what I normally do. So problem solved, right? I just need to get a couple more tips and I can take the subway back to the office. Still embarrassing, but the subway is full of odd characters so people will probably just think I'm a stripper on her way to a gig. In any case it'll get me back to the office a lot quicker.

I don't think I could pay the rent on street performing because it takes me another twenty minutes to collect two bucks. Once I do I stuff the rest of the flyers into the trash. My boss can fuck herself.

Not that I'm going to tell her that.

Out loud. In my head I tell her that all the time.

Besides, she's never going to know I tossed the rest of the flyers. Normally I wouldn't do something so unethical, but let's face it: I'm almost **certain** she made up this job just to get to me, and I did hand out most of them. Or more than half, which is most.

I wonder if the Budget Bridal Stop is even a client.

I bunch the material of the dress below my waist and lift it a few inches so I don't trip on it as I make my way down the subway steps so I can hop on the One towards the West Village. I buy a pay-per-ride card with my panhandling earnings and hold onto the quarter I have left over. Yay me.

According to the monitors the train is due to arrive in three minutes. I've been whistled at twice and received another offer for paid sex just in the time it took me to buy a ticket so I move as out of the way as possible and try to blend into the wall while I wait on the train's arrival.

I am sort of curious about the sex offer. Like I wonder what he wanted and how much he was willing to pay.

Not that I would have! Of course not. But it'd be nice to know how much I could fetch in a jam. Just saying.

The subways in New York have these incredible old tile mosaics spelling out the names of the stops. I find the workmanship so lovely in an age of neon signs and electronic monitors. They're so permanent in an era of disposability. I'm in the midst of examining the tiny tiles, marveling over how they must be near a hundred years old, when I feel someone beside me. When you live in the city you get pretty good at detecting people in your personal space versus just passing by, so I take a step to the right and turn, expecting another prostitution offer. I think I'm just gonna ask this time what kind of money we're talking about because I always imagined myself as a high-end call girl and not a twenty-dollar-blow-job hooker. I mean, if it ever came to that. It's like three back-up plans behind waitressing in Hawaii.

But it's not an offer for sex. It's the hottie from yesterday, grinning at me in all his dimpled glory.

Four

"So you're one of those girls," he says. His tone and expression are solemn as he shakes his head a little.

"Which girls?" I ask, confused.

"The crazy ones," he says with a laugh and drops his gaze to my dress. The dimples are in full force and his eyes are sparkling with mirth.

"Well, that's rude."

"How is that rude?" His brows fly up and he looks aghast in a teasing sort of way. "It was a compliment."

"How is calling someone crazy a compliment?" I narrow my eyes at him.

"Well, the crazy ones are usually good in bed."

"Well, I'm not," I say dismissively. Dick.

"You're not good in bed?" He tilts his head in my direction and lowers his voice. "Are you sure? I bet you've got crazy untapped sexual potential."

"No, I'm not crazy," I reply with a shake of my head but I can't help but smile. Untapped sexual potential? What a jackass.

"Of course not. It's just what? Wedding Wear Friday at your office?"

"Oh, I get it. You're one of those guys."

"Which guys?" he asks, but he's smiling.

"The asshole ones."

"Possibly." He nods. "I can't say it's never been mentioned."

"I bet."

The train pulls in and I move towards the doors as they open. Of course he follows. There's no reason to stand on that platform unless you're waiting on the next train, so I assumed he'd follow.

"Are you going to say yes?" he questions once we're onboard and the doors close. There are no seats available so I settle for slinging my elbow around a pole to steady myself as the train jerks into motion.

"No, I'm not interested in a threesome with you."

He throws his head back and laughs at that. He's stretched over me, his hands wrapped around the horizontal bar running over my head. I've got a view of his throat from this angle. The muscles flex as he laughs and I have to fight the urge to reach out and run my fingers along the collar of his shirt.

"At the altar. Are you going to say yes at the altar?"

Oh.

God, what an asshole. Is he ever going to ask me to three-way with him so I can turn him down?

"No, I'm not getting married today." I say married like it leaves a bad taste in my mouth, because it does. "And this isn't my dress. If I was getting married it wouldn't be in this. It'd be in…" I stop. "Not this." He doesn't need to hear more than that. "And I'd have done something more with my hair and I wouldn't be wearing sneakers." I thrust my foot out from underneath the hem of the dress and wiggle the toe of my shoe. "I'm wearing this stupid dress because I'm in the midst of a really bad day."

"I think you'd make a stunning bride just as you are."

I suck in my breath at that because he's staring at me

like he means it. What is his deal? Is he flirting with me or not? He has the bluest eyes I've ever seen on a man and it feels nice to have them trained on me. Plus he smells good and he makes me feel less stupid in this dress when he's standing beside me. As if it doesn't matter who stares because we're in on the joke together. Then he leans in closer and I think he might kiss me but his lips pause by my ear.

"And for the record, I'm not into threesomes. I like to focus my attention on one woman at a time." He eases back and meets my eyes while I suck in a breath.

"Don't you have a go-see or something to do?" I mutter because I'm blushing and I need to break this spell he has over me before I hump his leg on the subway.

"What's a go-see?" He looks confused.

"Isn't that what it's called? When you go see designers and they decide if they should book you or not?"

"You think I'm a model?" His eyes flash and his lips pull into a wide smile.

"I assumed you were," I say, eyeing his abs. He laughs at me so I snap my gaze back to his face. "But I meant like a runway model or something. You're obviously too hideous for print."

"Of course," he agrees.

The train slows as we pull into Penn Station and I tighten my arm around the pole so I don't stumble. He leans in closer as travelers push past to exit and new passengers enter, yet it's not intrusive. He's not taking advantage of the limited personal space available, which in New York is chivalry.

"So if you're not getting married today, do you want to tell me what the dress is about?" he asks when we're in motion again. "You don't even have a phone on you," he points out while eyeing the dress for a pocket that doesn't

23

exist. "That's not safe."

"Bad day at the office," I reply.

"Is your name really Lauren or was that a decoy name you give strange men?"

"It's really Lauren." I sigh. "I meant to give you my decoy name but you caught me off guard yesterday."

"Good. Lauren, have dinner with me tonight."

"I don't think so." And I really don't. He seems like the kind of guy who's way too much for me. And probably not the ideal guy to ease back into dating with. Like jumping on a stallion when you belong on one of those coin-operated ponies at the grocery store.

"Why not?"

"It's kinda last-minute," I offer because I don't have anything better.

"That's a weak excuse."

"I don't know you."

"How well do you know anyone?"

Good point.

"I'm trying to focus on my career right now." I say it firmly. It'd probably be more effective if I wasn't wearing a wedding dress in the middle of a workday. His eyes drop to the offending garment and then back to mine again before he speaks.

"How's that working out for you?"

"You know." I shrug. "It could be better, could be worse."

The train stops at Twenty-Eighth and we're quiet again as passengers jostle around us, exiting and entering.

"What about your girlfriend?" I ask when it's quiet again. I meet his eyes with a challenging stare while remembering the beautiful girl from yesterday. "She won't mind?"

"Don't be disgusting," he scoffs. "That vile creature

from yesterday was my sister. Now do you have any other assumptions about me that I need to correct? I'm not into threesomes. I'm not a model and I am most definitely not dating my sister." I raise my brows in challenge and he adds, "Or anyone who is not my sister."

"I just..." My eyes fall to his chest and I rub the palm of my free hand against my hip, bunching the material in my fist before releasing it. "I just don't know if I'm ready for you."

"It's just dinner, Lauren," he says and dammit if just his voice doesn't turn me on. "Say yes. You can wash your hair another night," he adds with his dimpled grin.

I tear my eyes from his mouth and wave a finger at him while narrowing my eyes. "I do actually need to wash my hair."

"Sure." He nods.

"And I have a book club meeting tonight."

"A book club meeting? On a Friday night?"

"It's a very progressive book club."

"Good. So they won't mind if I come."

"You want to come to my book club meeting?"

"Sure. Why not?"

"Um, because you haven't read the book?"

"That sounds pretty discriminatory coming from a progressive book club."

"That we'd require you read the book to attend?" I laugh.

"Maybe I'll buy the book after hearing it discussed. Did you ever think of that? You'd be doing the author a disservice by turning me away."

"But there will be spoilers. You'll know how it ends before you begin."

"Is that why you won't have dinner with me? Because you think you know how it ends before it even begins?"

He's right.

"Eight o'clock," I tell him. "We meet at the Book Bar on Seventh and Charles."

Five

I washed my hair.

I also shaved my legs… and everywhere else. Just in case. Because there is no possible way I'm sleeping with Max—a guy I met yesterday. If he even shows up, that is. He probably won't. He's probably some nutjob with a fetish for walking around the city making women swoon before he disappears. Trust me, it wouldn't even be the strangest fetish in this city.

But it never hurts to wash your hair. It needed to be done anyway, and it's hard to get extended bathroom time with four girls sharing an apartment so it's best to take advantage when you can. That's what I'm telling myself anyhow.

So it doesn't matter if he shows up or not. I washed my hair for me, not for the hot guy with the dimples and the flat stomach. The guy with the blue eyes, strong arms and dark hair. The one who managed to put a smile on my face during a really craptastic day.

God, I hope he shows up.

I'm wearing a white sundress. I think it's a funny nod to today's bridal dress fiasco, so why not? It's a knee-length dress with a bohemian vibe and spaghetti straps. I've paired it with strappy espadrilles and a blush-colored summer-weight cardigan.

As I examine myself in the mirror I wonder if this look is too sweet. I wonder if I should change into jeans and low-cut shirt. Or maybe a long skirt with a tank top. Or—fuck it. I look cute. Besides, I'm going to a book club meeting, not a date.

Right?

I stuff my eReader into my bag and leave my apartment. The elevator was fixed while I was at work, so my exit from the building is smoother than it was this morning. Maybe, just maybe, this day is going to end better than it started.

I hit the sidewalk and marvel in the wonder that is this city while I walk. It's not gotten hot yet and with the sun just about to set for the night, the temperature has dropped into a range for a perfect summer evening. The Book Bar is about a ten-minute walk from my apartment and I enjoy the walk. I'm used to walking most places now, something that would have been unfathomable to me when I lived in Iowa. I used to move my car from one end of the shopping center to the other.

But now I walk. And I love it. I love the people-watching and the noise. The sound of cabs honking has become almost meditative to me now. I pass restaurants with sidewalk seating, conversations spilling out along with the clink of cutlery. Drugstores with automatic doors swishing open and closed as people hurry in and out. There's a fervor of possibility everywhere you look here.

My book club meets at this really cool hybrid shop on Seventh. They sell wine and books—a Manhattan bookworm's dream. There's an area towards the back reserved for book club meetings. A couple of mismatched sofas and an odd assortment of chairs fill the space. They're covered in colorful pillows and there's a big beat-up coffee table in the middle of it all, the kind you can rest your feet on or spill a drop of red wine on and no one cares.

It's heaven tucked into the middle of the city.

My book club consists of an assortment of women of varying ages and backgrounds. At first glance you might not think we had anything in common, yet we unite once a month over a love of books and any surface differences we have melt away. Our group includes a nurse, a college student, and a real estate agent, just to name a few.

We're the first Friday group—romance novels. The shop hosts book clubs all the time, with different genres meeting on different weeks, different days. It's open to everyone—the store posts a schedule of what each group is reading so anyone can join in anytime.

Don't expect anything, I tell myself as I open the door to the Book Bar. *You're here for your book club, not a date. If he shows he shows. If he doesn't he doesn't. You don't need him to show in order to have a great night.*

There's a long bar just inside the door. Behind it is a cross between a bookshelf and a wine rack, alternating shelves of the books being featured this month and the wine being featured—they do a wine-of-the-month club here as well.

I don't see Max anywhere.

I wave at Martha—she's one of the owners and always here on Fridays—before I weave my way through the store towards the back, skirting the seating areas as I go. A line of bookshelves wall off the space where the book club meets, hiding it from the front of the store while creating a bit of privacy and keeping the noise down. Just off center there's a break in the bookcases, creating a doorway to get through. I take one last glance around the store for Max before I head through, reminding myself that I'm a few minutes early and I barely know the guy. He's probably got better things to do.

Or not.

Because he's here.

I bite my lip to hide the grin threatening to overtake my entire face as I observe him. He's sitting on the couch facing the doorway but he hasn't seen me walk in, his attention focused on the book in his hand. His legs are crossed, one foot on the opposite knee. One hand is holding the book and the other rubs lightly at his forehead as he reads.

Is there anything sexier than a man absorbed in a book? Not to this self-confessed book nerd there isn't. He's wearing jeans—a different pair than he had on earlier. These are darker and paired with a casual button-down in light blue, the sleeves rolled back to his elbows. His dark hair looks styled. I say that because it's not damp like it was yesterday or tousled like he'd run his hands through it when I saw him earlier today.

I want to rip his clothes off.

He flips a page as I watch him and his eyebrows rise at whatever is on the page. It's so cute. I wonder what he's reading? Wait. Oh, shit.

"You're reading the book," I blurt out.

He looks up, his face breaking into a smile when he sees me. "Of course I'm reading the book. I'm already on chapter eight."

"You didn't need to read the book," I mumble.

"You told me to read the book," he says as he stands. He's got a smirk on his face and he points at me as he says it.

"I think what I said was that it was odd to attend a book club meeting for a book you hadn't read. I didn't specifically tell you to read it."

"Well, at least now I know why you're so fixated on threesomes."

"Oh, God." I cover my eyes with my hand for a second before moving my fingers. "I'm not fixated. I'm not into that. I mean fictionally, yes, I'm into it. Really, really into it." He laughs and I drop my hand to my side and shrug. "But not really, not in reality," I add then trail off before meeting his eyes.

"Got it. Just a fantasy. You're not trying to recruit me into something kinky." He winks as he stands, picking up flowers I hadn't noticed lying beside him on the sofa and moving around the coffee table to stop in front of me. "I brought you this," he says, holding it out. "You didn't have one earlier."

I look down and take the flowers, a simple trio of pale pink peonies and a couple sprigs of eucalyptus. The stems are wrapped together with a jute twine. It's a tiny bridal bouquet—and possibly the sweetest gesture a man's ever made for me. He couldn't have bought these at a corner bodega on the way either, they're too specific. He found a florist to make a last-minute tiny bridal bouquet on a Friday afternoon in the height of wedding season in New York City. All to surprise a woman he barely knows.

"Thank you," I say softly, taking the flowers from him. I raise them to my nose, using them to hide the smile on my face.

"You're welcome," he replies and one of those damn dimples makes an appearance. "But don't use them to hide that smile of yours. It's captivating."

I drop the flowers down a few inches, the petals brushing against the exposed skin above my dress, and smile, twisting my lips after a second and laughing. "Thank you again," I say, glancing down at the flowers and back to him.

"I'll get us drinks," he says, gesturing towards the front. "What do you like?"

I'm tempted to say 'whatever you like' but I don't think he'd take that as an answer, so I ask for a Riesling then sit in the seat he vacated and pick up the paperback he left behind. I need a reminder about what happened within the first eight chapters so I flip it open to take a quick peek.

A lot happened.

He's turned down the corners on all the best—or worst, depending on how you look at it—parts. I'm turned on remembering those scenes, thinking about him reading those scenes.

Max returns with a bottle and two glasses as the women from my book club begin arriving, so I shut the book and place it on my lap, rubbing my fingers along the paper edge while I watch him pour each of us a glass and set the bottle on the table.

I am so sleeping with this guy if I get the chance.

Like the second I get the chance.

Does it make me a little whorish that I'm planning on getting him naked when I don't even know his last name? When we haven't so much as kissed yet?

I don't care.

He hands me a glass as he sits beside me on the sofa then rests his hand on my knee, drawing his thumb back and forth on my bare skin.

By the time he leans over to mention how great this place is I'm wet and I don't think he's even trying to turn me on. He just is.

Which leads me to fantasize about what Max is like when he's trying. Is he a hair-puller? A dirty talker? Would he want to bend me over and fuck me from behind or would he want to look into my eyes while I straddle him?

God, I hope this is a short meeting.

The rest of the girls arrive, dropping their bags and getting drinks. They're making small talk about the weather and dawdling and I wish they'd all hurry the fuck up.

As the meeting finally gets underway Max moves his hand from my knee. My skin instantly cools from the loss of his touch and I think I can probably keep my arousal in check for an hour as long as he's not touching me. But then he moves his arm to the back of the couch, his fingers resting on my shoulder, and I'm not so sure. When he winds a strand of my hair around his finger my nipples harden. He's not even tugging, not really, but holy fuck, just that tiny amount of having my hair played with is provocative as hell.

As the group starts a discussion about the decisions that lead the female lead to ask her lover to share her with another man, I place my hand on Max's thigh. I figure it's only fair to attempt to make him as crazy as he's making me.

He's wearing jeans. The well-worn denim is faded in all the right places and it's soft under my hand. I easily feel the heat of his skin and the contour of his muscles through the fabric and while I'm tempted to take this a lot farther, I'm well aware of where we are and that I don't want to get kicked out of book club for fondling my date during a meeting.

So I content myself with a light touch and the smallest squeeze of my fingertips.

I'm rewarded with a subtle tug at my hair in return.

A quick glance at the oversized clock hung behind the opposite sofa tells me it's only ten after eight.

I wonder how far he lives from here and if he has roommates. Please, for the love of me getting laid, let his roommates be out of town. Or at work. Hell, I don't even care if they're in jail, please just let them be anywhere but home tonight.

"Lauren?"

Sonia, one of my fellow book club members, is asking me a question. I imagine it's about the book we're here to discuss but I don't know because I was too busy thinking about places I can have sex with Max to listen.

"I'm sorry, what?" I ask, pulling my hand off of Max's thigh so I can concentrate. "What were you asking?"

"We're each sharing our favorite quote from the book. It's your turn," she says with a glance at Max.

Right.

I hand the paperback to Max and pull my eReader from my bag. "Just one second," I mumble as I open my device and click on my highlights. God, I can't read any of these out loud with Max sitting here. Did I highlight anything that isn't perverted? No. No, I did not. "You know," I say, snapping the cover of my eReader closed, "I think I'll pass this time and let Max read you his favorite instead."

The thing is I've had better ideas because Max doesn't miss a beat. Not a single one. No, he simply removes his arm from my shoulder and calmly flips the book open. I realize I've made a tactical error before he even begins speaking because just watching him handle the book is foreplay for me.

He thumbs through as he looks for a specific page he turned down. He's not hurried or nervous while he searches and I like the way he handles the book.

Wait, did I really just think that?

I did.

Reading is sexy, my friends. Very, very sexy.

The way his eyes scan the pages while he drags his bottom lip through his teeth. The way his fingers caress the edge of the book. The sound the pages make when he flips them and the almost inaudible whisper of his finger sliding down the page when he finds the section he's looking for.

Then he begins reading.

It's a part from the male's point of view. Where he asks Winnie—the female protagonist—to give him a chance. He promises that she can trust him with whatever her fantasy is and that he'll be careful with her. That he'll make it good.

I remember thinking at the time that my fantasy was a warm chocolate-chip cookie.

It's not now.

No, right now it's a man named Max. A really attractive man named Max with a voice that I could listen to all day long. A man I barely know, yet one who's brought me flowers and made me laugh. One I suspect looks just as good out of those clothes as he does in them.

I don't think I'm alone in my fantasies either because when he finishes speaking every member of my group is staring at him. There's a pause where no one says anything and then finally Debby speaks up and reminds Vilma that it's her turn to pick a favorite quote.

Max takes my hand during the remainder of the meeting and slowly rubs circles into my skin with his thumb. It's just my hand but it doesn't feel like it. It feels like he's caressing me everywhere. It feels like he's running his fingertips down my arm and up the inside of my thigh. If feels like my entire body is humming with his touch.

That's what it feels like.

Or I just have a really overactive sexual imagination.

Either way, when the meeting ends I stand up so fast my eReader hits the floor and I have to swoop down and pick it up. I shove it into my bag and then turn to Max.

"Are you ready?"

"Sure." He smiles at me and shakes his head a little as though he's surprised by my antsy demeanor. "I'm ready."

Six

"So, did you want to grab dinner?" Max asks once we're outside on the sidewalk.

"No." I might be looking at him like he's an idiot because who in the hell wants to eat right now?

"Okay." He shrugs. "I'll walk you home."

What?

"No, I'll walk *you* home," I snap back.

"You'll walk me home?" Max grins, dimples in full force. His eyes spark in amusement at my outburst. "How progressive of you."

"Yeah, I'm sort of revolutionary," I agree.

"Will you initiate the goodnight kiss as well?"

"Maybe." I shrug. "If you're lucky." I glance down the street, anxious to get moving. I start to ask him which way his place is but I don't get more than 'which' out of my mouth before his lips are on mine.

He's holding my face in both of his hands and brushing his lips gently over mine, a whisper of a touch a hundred times more skilled in its softness than I could have anticipated. "I am lucky," he murmurs, "but I also enjoy the occasional customs like flowers and first kisses. If that's okay with you."

"Yeah," I mumble because he's kissing me again.

"That's okay." It's way more than okay.

"Good." He tilts his forehead down to mine as he runs his hands down my upper arms. "Then let's go." He grabs my left hand and we begin walking south on Seventh, but as soon as we cross Eighteenth he hails a cab and holds the door for me before sliding in beside me. He gives the driver an address on Bleecker Street and I laugh.

"That's a mile from here," I point out. It's silly to take a cab a mile.

"I know," he replies with a wink. There's no more talking after that. There's no more talking because from that point on we're making out like teenagers in the back seat of a car. At one point Max lifts his hips and I think we're progressing to dry-humping but then I realize the cab has stopped and he's just trying to get cash from his wallet.

"You're walking me to the door, right?" he asks, kissing me again as he reaches over to push the cab door open. He's smiling as he asks. It's too dark and he's too close for me to see it, but I can feel his lips curve against my cheek. His skin is warm and rougher than my own and hell, yes, I'm walking him to the door.

"Of course I am. I don't just drop my dates at the door and speed off. I need to make sure you get inside safely." I shove him lightly with my hands as I speak because he's the one sitting on the sidewalk side of the cab and I'm anxious to get moving. Hello, can I be any more obvious?

Max steps onto the pavement and immediately takes my hand as I exit the cab, slamming the door behind me. It's a bit quieter on this street. Quieter for New York anyhow. There's a large residential building behind us and smaller three-story buildings, each made up of different shades of brick, directly across the street. Storefronts line the ground level of the buildings. It's quintessential New York City. Charming with a small-neighborhood feel. I think we're headed into the building behind us, but as the cab pulls away and the street clears Max walks me across and up to a door between a cosmetics store and a trendy women's clothing store.

As he inserts a key into the lock I place my hand on his arm, stopping him. "Wait, do you have roommates?"

His face falls and he shakes his head. "Shit, no, I'm sorry."

"You're sorry? Why?"

"I know how kinky you are." He sighs and leans his back against the door. "Did you want me to call a friend?"

"Shut up and open the door."

He grins and shoves open the door, walking backward into the stairwell and pulling me in after him. We're all over each other before the door has closed completely. I've abandoned my purse and the flowers and gotten his shirt half unbuttoned by the third step. His hand is under my dress by the sixth.

By the ninth I already know this is going to be the best sex I've ever had.

When we reach the landing I pull my dress over my head and drop it to the floor.

"Jesus, Lauren." Max groans as he runs his hands down my sides, his thumbs splaying over my skin. I fumble with the remaining buttons on Max's shirt before yanking it off of him, but I clearly missed one because the shirt catches then a button pings to the floor and skitters across the room.

"Oops, sorry," I offer.

"It's okay."

"Good, because I'm not that sorry."

39

He pinches my ass and I yelp.

"Sorry." He grins.

"No, you're not."

"I'm not," he agrees.

He picks me up and I wrap my legs around his waist. I have a fleeting thought that my ex wasn't strong enough to lift me and then I shove him from my mind because he doesn't matter anymore. Not in the slightest.

Max rests me on a hard surface I assume is the kitchen island and I shiver as he unsnaps my bra, his fingers trailing down my spine as the straps fall from my shoulders. I lift my hips as he hooks his fingers into my scrap of underwear and slides them over my hips to the floor.

"You're lovely," he murmurs as he drops his hands to the counter on each side of my hips and lowers his lips to mine.

"Ditto." I grin, eyeing his chest.

"There's that smile I'm so enamored with." He brushes his lips across mine. "But I'm going to wipe it off your face now."

"Yes, please."

"I like your enthusiasm."

"I like your cock."

"You haven't met my cock yet."

"I know, but you make me feel optimistic." I bite my lip as I say it because I realize it's true. He makes me feel hopeful. He makes me feel like me.

"Ditto," he repeats. His voice is soft and husky. His eyes are dark and piercing, his lips warm as they meet mine, soft yet firm. Perfect.

Outside a cab honks and someone shouts an obscenity. Inside Max's apartment I moan as he slips a finger inside of me. I groan when he makes it two and I clutch his forearms when he angles the heel of his hand over my clit.

"That's good," I gasp.

"I can do better than good," he says as he drops his head to my chest, his tongue flattening across one of my nipples. I love having my tits played with and when he moves his spare hand to my other nipple and tugs I clench around the fingers thrusting inside of me. Then he chuckles and adds teeth to the mix and I'm about done for.

"That's better than good," I pant, my breath short.

"You're quite the kinky girl for someone with such a sweet exterior." He withdraws his fingers from me and wraps his lips around them.

Fuck.

I watch him slide his fingers slowly out of his mouth, a light pop sounding when he's done. Then I'm scrambling off the counter and yanking at the button on his jeans, desperate to hold him, to feel him inside of me. Now.

"I'm not that sweet," I tell him as I free the button and tug at the zipper.

"Good to know," he replies and takes over with his pants, pushing my hands out of the way to free himself. His cock is hard. And sizable, oh, lucky day.

I am so glad I said yes to Max, I think as I wrap my hand around his cock. You can't go through life being skeptical just because you've been burned a few times. No one's intuition is right every time and I shouldn't blame myself for that. Besides, I think my instincts are improving because I feel really good about Max. I think I'm getting savvier because everything about this night is one big yes.

"Yes," he hisses as I twist my wrist and stroke the length of him.

See? We're in total harmony.

He wraps his hand over mine and we stroke him together. He's thick and long and I'm getting ever wetter feeling him in my hand. He really is long. I can't wait to sit on him.

"It is nice."

"It?"

"Your penis. I wasn't wrong." I flick my eyes to his and squeeze my hand around him.

"Thank you." He grins. "It's nice of you to mention. So polite," he adds with a smack to my ass which catches me off guard and I yelp. Then he lifts me again, my legs quickly wrapping around his waist, and moves us with ease to the sofa, resting me on my back and following me to the cushions.

It's leather and the material is smooth and cool beneath me, in stark contrast to the warmth and hardness above me. Max brushes a strand of hair off my cheek and kisses me. Our tongues swirl, exploring each other, before I press my lips to his neck, enjoying the texture of him—the subtle abrasiveness of his jaw, the skin rougher from shaving, growing softer the lower I explore. He smells like some combination of pine and the ocean, an expensive cologne, surely, but something else too. Something Max.

His pants are still hanging around his hips and I slide my hands inside and palm his ass, traversing the contours of his body, my hands behaving as though they're on a sexual voyage over the river and through the woods.

When I move to push his jeans lower my hand hits his wallet, so I pull it out, but I'm a terrible pickpocket because I immediately wave it in his face and ask if he's got a condom. Please let him have one in his wallet, because I don't think I can wait long enough for him to retrieve one from the bathroom or wherever the hell he stashes them.

Max nods as if to indicate for me to retrieve it myself, so I flip open the wallet while he watches, his mouth on my breast. On the left side there's a New York driver's license in a clear window telling me Max the non-model somehow still manages to take a great ID photo, which everyone knows is near impossible, and that his name is Max Hunter. I smile at that because I didn't know his last name till just this second. On the right side of the wallet are three credit cards in staggered slots and behind that one long pocket for cash. I dig my finger behind his license and am rewarded with not one, but two condoms.

"Two," I say, holding them up and tossing the wallet aside. "I like your confidence."

"I hope you still like it tomorrow when you have trouble walking."

"Oh, game on." I rip one of the condoms open and examine it in the dim light to make sure I have it flipped the right way and then slide one hand up the length of him while placing the condom on him with the other.

I roll it down slowly, inch by inch. His cock is hard and heavy in my hand, the condom slick. When I've finished I turn my eyes to his while placing my palm on his abs, lightly scratching with my fingernails. Then I yelp as he slides me lower on the couch while spreading my thighs wide and settling between them. He maneuvers me like I weigh nothing, positioning me to his liking. He's got one of my legs over his shoulder and the other resting in the crook of his arm. Then he guides himself to my entrance and slaps me with his dick. He does it again and I groan.

"Stop fucking with me and put it inside."

"You want it inside?" he teases, nudging his tip at my entrance.

"Yes." I arch my back and grip the armrest over my head. "Yes, dammit. Now."

"I don't know," he says, pausing and easing back. "I'm not sure. Do you think we're ready for this, Lauren? Maybe we should wait?"

"Are you kidding me right now?" I move my arms back and slap them against the couch, trying to pull myself up enough to argue with him. I'm dripping on his sofa and he's playing hard to get. Unreal. I knew he was too good to be true. This city is filled with weirdos. Hot, dimpled, sex-withholding weirdos. It's probably his fetish, getting women worked up and spread eagled on his sofa. Teasing them about how good it's going to be and making promises about being unable to walk after and then not delivering. Son of a bitch.

"Yes, I'm kidding," he says, and then he confirms it when he slides into me in one long thrust.

One hard thrust. Perfectly positioned.

A thrust that stretches me with the most delicious ache.

It's perfect.

He's perfect.

He slaps my tits lightly and then pinches my nipples simultaneously. Quick, rough and unexpected. I bow my back off the sofa and scream his name.

"I'm going to fuck these next, Lauren," he says while gripping my tits so hard I wonder if they'll bruise. I don't care if they do—totally worth it. Every touch and pinch and pull makes me wetter, my nipples a direct ticket to my arousal. I squeeze around his cock in rhythm to his thrusting and squeeze harder when he does.

"So good, Max. So good. Just like that." I should be shocked by my wanton behavior with him. Or have a moment of modesty over the sounds we're making—the slapping of skin and the sound of his cock sliding in and out of me. The indeterminate sounds coming from my mouth and the dirty words coming from his. The mess we are surely making on his couch.

But I'm not. All I care about is how good this feels. The pressure building in my pelvis. The heat, the sweat, the way it feels when he leans forward enough to cause contact with my clit as he brushes his lips across mine. The words he whispers about how beautiful I am and how good it feels to be inside of me. The way he tugs my hair to position my neck for his mouth.

That's all that's on my mind right now.

"I'm close," I tell him, but he shakes his head and shifts his hips, sliding out of me.

"No."

"What do you mean no? I want to come!" I whine.

"Not yet."

"What do you mean not yet? Can't you catch up?" Then I mouth the word 'please' silently and he laughs.

"Good things come to those who wait, Lauren."

"The early bird gets to come, Max."

"Jesus," he says, but he's grinning. "I should have been paying more attention to women who read. Who knew that bookworms were so mouthy in bed?"

"I can read aloud to you later if you want," I offer with a wink.

"Like a kinky bedtime story?" He looks interested.

I nod, my hair sliding against the leather beneath me.

"Okay, deal," he agrees half a second before he slams into me again. I grunt as the air is knocked out of me and then brace my hands over my head against the arm of the sofa as he moves.

"Max," I cry and arch my back. It's too good. And when he pinches my nipples again I climax, my muscles contracting around him like a vise. Above me his shoulders jerk as he comes and he licks his lip as his mouth opens on a pant. It's sexy as hell and I pulse around his cock again, an aftershock to my orgasm.

If it's possible to glow from sex, I'd swear I'm glowing. It's probably just sweat but I'm going to enjoy my moment.

He pulls out and then flips us so I'm lying on top of him, both of our chests heaving. I close my eyes for a moment and lay my head down while he runs his fingers through my hair.

"Max?"

"Hm?"

"I need to get up."

"In a minute."

"I'm dripping on your thigh though."

"I know," he agrees and slides his other hand down my back and cups my ass, holding me to him.

"You're going to have a stain on your couch."

"God, I hope so. I'll think of you every time I jerk myself off while looking at it."

"How sweet," I reply, propping my chin on my hand to look at him.

"Question," he states by way of asking.

"What?" I examine him from beneath my lashes, wondering what he wants to know.

"Now can I buy you dinner? I'm starving."

"Yes," I laugh, pushing myself to a sitting position and finally looking around. Exposed brick and industrial ductwork. Huge kitchen with, yes, a large marble-covered island that my ass was on. Stainless appliances and open shelving and... stairs? "You have a second floor?" I question.

"Yeah, but don't go up there."

"Why not?" I ask and the skepticism must be written all over my face because he laughs.

"God, you're easy. I'm kidding. My bedroom is up there. Go clean up and find something to wear. I'll order dinner."

"You're just going to send me to your bedroom unaccompanied?"

"Yup. Go ahead and snoop, Snooper McSnooperton."

"Snooper McSnooperton?"

"Do you prefer Curious Kitty? Nosey Night Owl?"

"I'll take Nosey Night Owl."

"Deal."

"I'm just not used to so much transparency," I add.

"You've got trust issues or something?"

"No. More like issues with my judgment."

"Because you hang out with jackasses?"

"Yeah something like that."

He gets up and pulls on his pants as he walks to the kitchen. Opening a drawer, he holds up a menu and asks if Chinese is okay.

"Ohhh!" I clap my hands together in excitement. "We're ordering Chinese?"

He walks back over, handing me his shirt and the menu, then jogs down the stairs to retrieve everything I abandoned on the way up. "What do you want?" he asks, thumbing through his phone, his thumb poised over the dial.

"I can't decide." I tap my finger against my lip. This is exciting for me. Like for real exciting. Big deal exciting. My stomach grumbles.

"Between?" He hits dial and raises the phone to his ear.

"The Mongolian beef or the sesame chicken," I muse. "Or maybe the lo mein. Do they have good egg rolls?" I squeak as he begins speaking into the receiver. "Hold on, hold on, I'll decide!" I tell him but he waves me off and orders everything I just mentioned, plus a chicken with broccoli.

Obviously, I'm in love with him.

Just kidding, I'm not quite that easy.

I run upstairs and clean myself up while we wait for the food, but I keep his shirt on because I like it. Also because I couldn't find anything better to wear when I snooped. I considered one of his t-shirts, but they were clean and the shirt I'm wearing smells like Max. He's got a lot of nice clothing though. Suits and silk ties. This apartment. He's clearly not in entry-level marketing.

The doorbell rings, so I abandon my snooping and head back downstairs. I arrive to Max spreading our feast out on the island.

"Tell me you cleaned that countertop," I quip as I snag an egg roll. "Holy crap, I'm going to eat everything," I mumble with my mouth full. "So good," I add and take a seat on a bar stool. "Thank you for dinner. All the dinners, since you ordered three of them for me."

"You're welcome, but I did it for myself."

"How so?" I ask, dragging the containers of food closer to me and eyeing him.

"I need you to keep your energy up. For the sex marathon."

"I'm going to be too full to have sex after eating all this food." I wave a fork over my spread and shrug. "So I hope *Sex Marathon* is the name of a show you wanted to watch together."

He drags two of the containers back towards him.

"What do you do anyway?" I ask, glancing around his apartment.

"Finance."

"Ugh, finance guys are the worst. My ex is in finance."

"Lauren, the only ex here is the X-cross in my sex room down the hall."

"Really?" My eyes bug out.

"No, not really." He shakes his head while looking at me like I'm crazy. "There's an office and another bathroom at the end of the hall."

"Holy shit, you have two bathrooms?"

"Should I have led with that when I asked you out?" He gets up and pulls bottled waters out of the oversized stainless refrigerator and hands one to me. "Two bathrooms and Chinese delivery is the way to your heart. Got it."

"Hell, yes, you should have led with that. Two bathrooms in New York City? I share one bathroom with three other girls. The idea of two bathrooms all to myself might make me spontaneously orgasm." I wave a hand over my face. "Is it hot in here?"

"We can fuck in both of the bathrooms if you're into it," he offers.

"Do go on." I stuff a forkful of noodles into my mouth and nod.

"I've got one hell of a walk-in shower in the bathroom upstairs."

"Hmmm."

"Italian Carrera tile." He drops his voice and raises his eyebrows suggestively. "Basketweave mosaic," he adds with a wink.

I laugh. "I already checked your bathroom out. You've got a herringbone tile not a basketweave."

"Do you think I have any idea what I'm saying? I'm just spouting words I think are going to turn you on. Subway tile, Egyptian cotton, rainfall shower head. Is any of this working?"

"Oh, it's working, but it's unnecessary. You had me at two bathrooms, remember?"

"Never hurts to load the bases."

Seven

We're almost finished eating when I spot the fortune cookies left scattered by the takeout bag. "Look, they gave us extra fortune cookies!" I squeak, eyeing the pile.

"Well, to be fair, we ordered enough food for half a dozen people so I think they gave us a normal amount," Max comments wryly, but he seems amused by my excitement, his eyes lingering on my face.

"Hush," I tell him as I grab one. I crack it open, eat one corner of the cookie then pull out the fortune and read it aloud. "'You are capable, competent, creative and careful.'" I nod and place the fortune on the counter. "Now you go," I tell Max.

He pops a piece of broccoli in his mouth as he opens one of the plastic-sealed cookies and cracks it open. "'You will be invited to a small gathering with spicy conversation,'" he reads with a smirk. "Well, this one has already come true," he comments as he eyes me in his shirt.

"Okay, my turn." I grab another cookie and pop the package.

"You didn't finish the last one." Max points his fork at the abandoned fortune cookie pieces lying on his countertop.

"I know, I just like the fortunes," I tell him, but I eat a piece of the new cookie as I unfurl the paper. "'Time is the wisest counselor,'" I read off. We both groan and I toss it on the counter. "Boring. Your turn."

Max pops another cookie open and glances at the paper with a grin. "'The object of your desire comes closer,'" he reads and then suggestively looks me over.

"You keep getting the good ones," I mumble as I grab another, again eating one bite of the new cookie as I flip the paper around so I can read it. "'You find beauty in ordinary things. Do not lose this ability,'" I read from the paper. "Eh, kinda generic."

"Why do you keep doing that?" Max asks.

"Doing what?"

"Eating part of each cookie. Why don't you just finish one of them?"

"I don't really want the cookie, but I feel like it's bad luck if I don't eat at least part of it before I read the fortune."

"What about my luck? You didn't let me in on this little superstition and now my fortunes are invalid!" He waves at the uneaten cookies in front of him and glares at me.

"Yours aren't!" I insist. "It's my superstition, it doesn't apply to you!"

"But how could you risk it, Lauren?" He looks at me so beseechingly I can't help but laugh. His eyes are so imploring. I think he could get me to do just about anything with those eyes.

"Okay, I'm sorry! I apologize. I was wrong not to tell you about the proper procedure for eating and reading a fortune cookie."

"Apology accepted, but I've got my eye on you."

I roll my eyes and shrug, "Last one's yours," I tell him

and slide the remaining cookie across the counter.

He opens the package and makes a big show of stuffing half the cookie in his mouth before reading the fortune. Then his brows draw and he nods to himself before stuffing the rest of the cookie into his mouth and the slip of paper into his pocket.

"You're not going to read it?" I question, confused.

"I read it."

"You're not going to read it to me?" I try again, a little hurt. Why do I feel like things just got weird?

"I'm saving it for later," he says and I wonder what the hell that means.

"Um, okay," I agree without looking at him and sweep up the mess of cookie crumbs onto my plate while wondering if all men are covert or just the ones I'm attracted to. "That's really cagey," I blurt out.

"Cagey? How am I cagey?" He looks so confused I second-guess my gut reaction to question him. Why am I so suspicious? "We're in my apartment and I gave you carte blanche to go through my stuff. You're the one who wouldn't let me walk you home," he points out as he gets up and drops our plates into the dishwasher. Bastard has a dishwasher too.

"Oh, that." Yeah, he has a point. "That's because I share a one-bedroom apartment with three other girls."

"How does that work exactly?" He looks genuinely curious, then grins. "Does it involve snuggling and pillow fights?"

"No, pervert. Bunk beds."

"Bunk beds," he repeats with a nod, but then a moment later he frowns, subtly, the skin on his forehead wrinkling for a fraction of a second, so quick I wonder if I imagined it. "Can I get you anything else to drink? Should I open a bottle?" He's not facing me, sticking leftovers in the fridge as he asks, and I wonder if it's a dismissal. I wasn't expecting to spend the night here. I wasn't expecting to be here at all, but then he showed up for my book club with his dimples and flowers and things got out of hand.

"Do you want me to leave? It's getting late." I should probably go before I fall for this guy. This has gone too far—time to shield myself.

"No, I definitely don't want you to leave." He pops his head around the fridge door and stares at me. "What's this talk of leaving?"

"Um, I don't know."

"You promised me a dirty bedtime story," he reminds me. "You're staying."

"Okay." I grin, the weirdness from before forgotten.

"I think I've got something you'll like," he says as he pulls a bottle from an under-counter wine fridge and sets it on the counter before peeling the seal off and grabbing a corkscrew. He's really adept with a corkscrew and I'm intoxicated watching the muscles in his arms flex as he grips the bottle and pops the cork. Adeptness is a turn-on, even for a simple task. "Where'd you say you were from, Lauren?"

"I didn't say."

He tilts his head as if to ask the question now.

"You don't think I'm a New Yorker born and raised?" I ask with a laugh.

"Not quite." He shakes his head as he pours the first glass.

"Iowa," I tell him.

"Iowa." He repeats it slowly for such a short word. "What brought you to New York?"

"A guy." I take the offered glass and bring it to my lips. "The stupid finance guy."

"The cheater," he says, focused on tilting the bottle, pouring a glass for himself.

"Yeah." I nod. "That he was." I pause for a moment, thinking. "Wait, when did I mention that he cheated on me?" I don't remember mentioning it. I find it sort of embarrassing so I'm usually careful about who I mention it to.

"This afternoon. When you tried to get out of having dinner with me." He flashes a smile at me while stowing the half-full bottle in the fridge.

"I did? Oh, that's weird. I try not to mention it. But yeah, he was a cheater. Is still a cheater, I assume. He's just cheating on someone else now, I suppose."

"He's an idiot," Max snaps. "You shouldn't blame yourself."

"That's true," I agree. "But it's hard not to. For a long time I felt stupid for not seeing it, you know? But hell, I was in Iowa most of the time it was going on." I shrug. "So now I blame his friends."

"Why's that?" Max asks, pausing.

"So I don't have to blame myself?" I joke. "Because he was a pretty nice guy in college. Then he came to New York and got a fancy job and a nice apartment and I don't know what happened to him. He changed. Started hanging out with a bunch of Wall Street types. No offense," I add when he raises a brow at that comment.

"I'll let it pass."

"His friends are clearly a bunch of degenerate douchebags though. You'd think just one of them might have pointed out to him that he already had a girlfriend."

"Maybe they didn't know."

"Possibly." I nod. "Except he actually told me it wasn't a big deal. Said he was just blowing off steam and that I got to be his girlfriend. Like I should be honored I got top billing in a polygamous relationship I wasn't aware I was in." I snort.

"Huh," he murmurs.

"You don't hang out with guys like that, right?" I question.

"Not on purpose, no," he says, then adds, "Fuck him," as he pulls me off the stool I'm on and leads me back to the couch we had sex on before dinner. Then we talk and kiss and it's the best night of my life. He asks questions about my job and my roommates and what I miss about home and what I like most about the city.

He agrees my boss is a troll and listens to all of the ideas I would have liked to have implemented for Budget Bridal instead of walking around Times Square in a wedding dress today.

We just really hit it off, like we've known each other forever.

Later we go upstairs and Max gets that bedtime story.

"Once upon a time there was a girl named Lauren and her mouth was so, so wet," I purr into his ear as I slide my hand lower.

"Fuck," Max groans in response. He doesn't say much after that. After all, it's my story.

Eight

On Monday I smile my way through the entire day. I spent the weekend with Max, returning to my apartment only long enough to grab clean clothes on Saturday morning and not returning again until Sunday night. We played tourist all weekend, doing the things I imagined I'd do when I moved here. We saw a show on Broadway, something Brad had kept promising to do with me but never had. After, we walked through Times Square, which is insane twenty-four hours a day, but at night it's insane with a neon cherry on top. There's nothing like Manhattan at night. The lights, the sounds, the energy, the people.

We got gyros from a street vendor on Fifty-Third and Sixth that Max insisted would change my life and edible cookie dough from the new place in Greenwich Village that I contended would change the size of my ass. Max whispered some very filthy promises to me about how we'd burn the calories off while we waited in a line that snaked out the front door and down the block.

We even took one of those double-decker bus tours. Max said he'd never been on one either—and it was probably pretty repetitive for him to see a bunch of sites he's seen for years, but we went anyway. We took a night tour and I know it's silly because we were on a bus and surrounded by tourists, but it was romantic. Like stupid romantic. Max had his arm slung around me as I rested my head on his shoulder and enjoyed the tour. We drove past Rockefeller Center and Madison Square Garden. Past the Empire State Building illuminated in white light and the Flatiron Building, which the tour guide told us was mocked upon completion by critics believing the combination of the triangular shape and height would cause the building to fall down. Over a hundred years later it still stands and is considered one of the most photographed buildings in the world.

We crossed the Brooklyn Bridge, which is stunning in the daylight and magic after dark, the lights running up the cables to the top of the stone towers and then back down again. On the Brooklyn side of the bridge the bus stopped long enough for picture-taking of the Manhattan skyline. Max took our picture with his phone, smiles on our faces and the city sparkling behind us. My heart beats a little faster and I suck my lip between my teeth just remembering it.

I'm so happy even my troll boss hasn't been able to get me down. She keeps looking at me suspiciously, likely trying to imagine what's making me happy so she can dream up ways to squash me, but whatever. It doesn't matter. She doesn't matter because I will find another job eventually. This job is just a blip on the radar of my career. I've already found two open positions within the company that I'm perfect for and applied. Maybe I'll get one of them, maybe I won't. But eventually I'll find something because I won't quit until I do.

It turns out I don't have to wait very long because on the following week I get asked to interview for one of the jobs I applied for and I have an offer by the end of the week.

It's to move to the social media team. A twenty percent increase in pay and, even better, it's a job I could be excited about doing. I really clicked with the supervisor I interviewed with. She's a blogger too and we spent most of the interview chatting about affiliate programs and algorithms. She blogs about living in small spaces and when I told her about my bunk bed living situation she asked if she could take some photos and feature my apartment on her blog. So, yeah, we totally hit it off and—dare I be too optimistic?—I think she's going to be more than a boss, I think she's going to be a friend too. She's already sent me links to several blogging conferences she wants me to attend and told me if there's any others I'm interested in to let her know, that as long as it's something I can use for work then we can find a way to justify sending me. It's a dream gig. I'll be using my skills instead of wearing a wedding dress in Times Square and I'll be getting paid to learn things that I'll also be able to apply to my personal blog.

You know that saying about how fast life moves? That in the blink of an eye everything can change? It's true. I've spent the last year stuck, so to say, and these past two weeks it feels as if my life is moving faster than a New York minute.

Probably because it is. A promotion and a new guy. Crazy.

And not just any guy. The perfect guy.

One who makes me smile.

One who makes me shelve my skepticism.

One I might be falling in love with.

I know it's only been a couple of weeks. I know it sounds insane and like I should use more caution. But it feels right. It feels like everything is coming together. Meeting Max feels like the reason I came to New York. I mean, I know the reason I came to New York was Brad. But when that went south, I stayed. I persevered though a shitty year at work and a tight budget. Through self-doubts and questioning if I should have gone back to Iowa with my tail between my legs where I could have at least afforded my own apartment and a car. But I didn't. I stayed and meeting Max is more than a reward for staying. Max is like the answer to everything happens for a reason. Like all roads led to him. So cheesy, but I don't know how else to explain it.

I'm still smiling when I walk through the door after work on Friday and the entire time I get ready.

"You're seeing the new guy again tonight?"

"Yup," I reply with a big grin on my face.

My roommate Allison—the part-time fit model—is sitting on the couch in our apartment watching me get ready at our kitchen table-turned-vanity.

"Where are you going?"

"We're having dinner with his sister. Some Indian restaurant that she loves and Max tolerates."

"His sister, huh? Serious stuff." Allison looks up from her phone with interest, my love life suddenly becoming more interesting than her social media. "Didn't you just meet this guy?"

"Yeah, a couple weeks ago. But what can I say? I like him."

"I like him too," Allison comments.

"You haven't met him." I turn to her in confusion, mascara wand halfway to my lashes.

"I like that he keeps you at his place all weekend. Last weekend you were gone, Delaney flew home for someone's wedding and Bridget was on a multi-night leg with the airline. I took a ten-minute shower on both Saturday and Sunday and pretended I lived alone. It was glorious." She sighs happily.

"Did I tell you Max has two bathrooms?" I finish with the mascara and apply my fade-resistant lipstick.

"Two? Marry him."

"I know, right?" I nod. "But all joking aside, I really like him."

"Well, if you like him I like him too," Allison says from the sofa, where she makes a big production of stretching out and hogging the entire sofa. "I think I'm gonna watch a movie on my laptop tonight. Without headphones. Bam," she boasts as she kicks back.

I laugh because I know what she means. When you have roommates you spend a lot of time with headphones shoved in your ears so you're not disturbing the others. "Enjoy your movie with the added soundtrack of the neighbors downstairs having sex and the ones across the hall fighting."

"Oh, I will." Allison claps her hands in glee. "Neighbor noise equals bonus soundtrack," she says while scrolling through the options on her laptop.

A minute later Max arrives, the buzzer from the front door announcing his arrival. Allison hops off the couch before I've even set my hairbrush down and hits the release, allowing him into the building. Then she opens the front door and leans into the hallway waiting on his arrival like a little sister about to check out her sibling's big date.

"You're way too excited about my social life, Allison," I comment.

"I'm bored. Sue me," she retorts.

I'm about to ask her why she's home for the second weekend in a row, as it's not like her, but Max is here so I slip my feet into a pair of sandals and fasten the straps while introducing them.

Allison takes an instant liking to him, meaning she grills him for info.

"What are your intentions towards my friend?" she asks exactly one heartbeat after introductions are made.

Max laughs and I roll my eyes. I don't have to tell Max she's joking because she can't keep a straight face herself, bursting into a fit of giggles the moment the words are out of her mouth.

"Sorry, I don't know where that came from," she says between giggles. "I just channeled my dad for a minute there."

"Well, rest assured, I've only the kinkiest of intentions towards Lauren."

"Lucky bitch," Allison mutters and we all laugh while I grab my purse.

"Don't forget your stuff," Max tells me as I raise a brow in question. "Weekend bag? I'm not bringing you home," he murmurs into my ear as he pulls me close and kisses the spot just under my ear.

I was hoping I'd be spending the weekend with him again, but I didn't want to be presumptuous, so I've only mentally packed a bag. As in I know exactly what I need to grab right now and even which bag I'm bringing, but I haven't actually packed the bag.

"Okay," I agree with a quick nod. "Just give me a second to grab some things," I tell him as I dash into the bedroom to grab my bag and the predetermined outfits for the weekend. Max stands in the doorway and watches me with an amused expression on his face.

"You're packing pretty fast there, tiger."

"Yeah, because I'm starving and we're going to be late for dinner," I lie.

"No rush, my sister is rarely on time."

"I'm ready," I announce half a second later and he does nothing to hide his smirk as he walks into the room.

"The infamous bunk beds," he comments as he takes the bag from my hand. "Which one's yours?"

"Top bunk," I say, patting the side of the mattress.

"We can play top bunk later if you want." He winks at me and I laugh while pushing at his chest and directing him towards the door. I grab my makeup bag as we pass the kitchen table. I've already got a toothbrush at Max's. He gave me a spot for it and everything. He bought me shampoo and conditioner last weekend too. He'd complained that my hair didn't smell like vanilla when I used the stuff in his shower and then ordered the stuff I normally use and had it delivered the same day. Manhattan is great for indulgent same-day delivery. Full-size bottles. His walk-in shower has two recessed niches for shampoo bottles and he gave one of them to me.

Who says chivalry is dead?

Toiletry space in the shower is a really big deal.

Nine

Max's sister is great. She is late, he wasn't wrong about that. She bursts into the restaurant at quarter past eight with a big smile and apologies for her tardiness. She's a student at NYU and full of bright-eyed optimism about humanity and the future. She waves her hands around when she talks and casually tosses out that Max and I would make cute babies midway through dinner. She says it like it's fact and with an offhand sincerity, not as if she's trying to cause trouble or rile Max up.

"Thank you, Molly. I haven't had the chance to talk to Lauren about knocking her up yet but now seems as good a time as any," Max deadpans while I enjoy watching their interactions. I'm an only child so this sort of sibling banter is new to me. "Lauren," he begins as he places his hand over mine on the table. "Would you like to have my children? I was thinking five with exactly twenty-six months between each, so we should probably get started sooner rather than later. Perhaps tonight, if you're ovulating."

"Five? In the city?" I widen my eyes in response. "Not unless you have a third floor I didn't notice."

"Don't be ridiculous. We'll move to Connecticut between the second and third child. I've already put a

65

deposit down on Max Junior's future preschool. The good ones book up before birth. Everyone knows that."

"Of course," I agree. "But how do you know the first will be a Max?"

"Max, Maxine. Either or."

"Huh." I shrug. "Well, I have some reservations about having five of them, but it sounds like you've already thought this through so why not."

"Okay, okay, enough, you two. Now you're grossing me out," Molly protests.

"You asked for it," Max says, pointing at her with a piece of naan before ripping a piece off and stuffing it into his mouth. But he does it kindly and with humor. I love that about him. The way he treats his sister. The way he glances behind me every time he holds a door open to make sure there's not another woman within a ten-foot radius he should keep holding the door for. It's so freaking archaic, and he doesn't even realize he's doing it—and I love it. I love that in a city of haste he never seems rushed when he's around me. I know he's got a stressful job—he works in venture capitalism just like Brad did. So I know it can be brutal and the hours long, but he leaves it at the office. Yes, I've seen him pull out his laptop on the weekends to catch up on something, but he never makes me feel like I'm in the way. When he's around me his focus is me and it's sexy as hell.

The way he flirts with me and how he makes me laugh all the time. The way he makes sure I have my shampoo at his place and how he walks on the outside of the sidewalk because he wants to be between me and the street. He makes me feel protected when I didn't even realize I was missing that feeling.

Don't even get me started on the sex. Raw and dirty and good. Uninhibited, messy. He makes me laugh and makes me come. Yet as good as it is—as great as it is—we fit together in so many other ways too.

It occurs to me then that I love a lot of things about him and my stomach tightens. I swore I'd never get this lost in a guy again, but here I am tumbling into love like an idiot.

"Anyway," Molly interjects. "Are you bringing Lauren to the Hamptons for the fourth? You're still coming, right?"

"Yes, we'll be there," he tells her. "And we're taking the pool house."

"You've got a pool house?" I question. I knew about the Hamptons house. It belongs to his father but according to Max he never uses it anymore. I knew we'd be sharing it with his sister, but I was envisioning a shore house filled with beds and dated appliances.

"You haven't been?" Molly questions. "You're going to love it. It's only a couple hours outside of the city and it's a breath of fresh air during the summer. You know how the city gets," she says, scrunching her eyebrows, "all hot and stinky and extra-crowded. We're on the beach if you prefer salt water to chlorine."

"You've got a beach," I repeat with a glance at Max. "And a pool."

"Oh! We'll get ice cream!" Molly continues. "I'll take you to the Fudge Company! They have the best soft serve." Molly claps her hands in excitement. "And candy!"

"What are you, ten?" Max interjects.

"No, I'm just excited you're bringing someone this year who won't hit on my friends," she retorts while shooting him a dirty look. "And you can have the pool house," she adds with a sweet smile. "You should enjoy it while you can. Once you have all those kids you'll have to stay with them in the main house."

"Touché, little sister."

***

Later as we're walking back to Max's apartment he apologizes for Molly's enthusiasm.

"It's okay, I already knew something must be wrong with you."

"Yeah, that I'm related to a crazy person. Don't worry about our future children though. Molly's adopted."

"She is not," I say, laughing while I elbow him in the ribs. "She looks exactly like you."

"Fine, that's a lie." He sighs. "She's my sister. And not even a half-sister."

"I like her."

"Yeah, I like her too." He grins and throws an arm around my shoulders. "So you're looking for things that are wrong with me, huh?"

"Absolutely." I nod. "You're too perfect to be real."

"I really am," he agrees.

"So what is it then, Prince Charming? Gambling debts? An arrest record? A shaky psychiatric past, maybe? You can't possibly have a wife or girlfriend tucked away somewhere, since you've introduced me to your sister."

"No wives. And no girlfriends except yourself," he adds, grabbing my hand as we cross Eleventh Street. It's probably not very mature, but my heart beats a little faster hearing him refer to me as his girlfriend. "I gamble during the occasional guys' trip to Atlantic City, but I can take it or leave it. I narrowly avoided arrest a couple of times in college, but my record is officially clean. And though I haven't been professionally evaluated, I think my psyche is sound."

"So what about me? Aren't you wondering what my crazy is? Everyone's got some, right? This is still new," I say, gesturing between us. "Maybe I'm just on my best behavior."

"No, I'm not worried." We're standing at the corner of Perry and Hudson, waiting for the light to change so we can cross. He looks me in the eyes when he says it and I think I might swoon on the damn sidewalk, which while romantic is really unappealing because the sidewalks in Manhattan are generally pretty filthy. Then he adds, "I already know what your crazy is."

"What do you think you know?" I ask, narrowing my eyes.

"You get a little nuts if the cream in your morning coffee isn't just so. You pour it in and stir it," he says, mimicking a spoon with his hand. "And then you pour in another drop and stir it again. Every time."

"Fine," I huff. It's true.

"And you panic about running out of cream when you've just opened a brand-new bottle."

"An heir and a spare."

"What?" He glances at me as we walk. "What does that even mean?"

"Royalty? They always have to have an heir to the throne, right? And then they need to have a second in case something happens to the first. So it's an heir and a spare."

"That's fucked up."

"Says the guy who wants five kids."

"What does this have to do with coffee creamer?"

"Oh! I like a spare bottle. Once the main bottle is open, I like to see the spare lined up in the fridge."

"Right." He nods. "Not crazy. I'm two hundred steps from a corner bodega, but a spare bottle of creamer is cause for panic."

"I just really like for my morning cup of coffee to go the right way."

"Next. If you eat more than half a bag of gummy bears it hurts your stomach, but you never stop at half a bag. You eat the entire bag and then complain for at least an hour about how much your stomach hurts."

"Oh, that." I shrug. "That's just part of my charm."

"It's something," he agrees.

"So you want to take me to the Hamptons instead of the friends who flirt with girls barely out of high school?" I joke because I have a way of ruining a perfectly good moment.

He glances at the timer next to the traffic light. They have them at every intersection of New York, it seems— a small neon light counting down the seconds until impatient pedestrians can cross and then the clock resets again. The tourists I've noted will generally wait for the traffic light to give them permission to cross before stepping into the street. Locals are more likely to step off the curb the moment the last car has spun past.

"Guys from work," he says with a shrug. "I didn't realize they were that bad. Or maybe I did," he adds. "Maybe I should have."

"I'm sorry," I say. "I'm being rude."

"You're fine."

"Can I ask you something?"

"You can ask me anything."

"Forget it, it's going to come out weird." I change my mind as I swing our joined hands together as we walk down Hudson.

"It can't be weirder than a conversation about how cute our future children are going to be."

"So that," I start because that's what I want to ask him

about. "Do guys really think about that stuff?"

"What stuff? Having a family? Some guys do. I do."

"Huh," I say, because honestly it surprises me a little. Men have always been a bit of a mystery to me in that regard. I assumed women were the ones who thought about babies and school districts and just sort of dragged the men along. When I was engaged I was the one who did all the planning, and I thought that was normal. Not that we got very far into it anyway.

"Guys worthy of your time think about that stuff."

"Worthy of my time. I like that. So full disclosure," I say, drawing in a breath. "You remember that I was engaged before?"

"Yeah," he replies, squeezing my hand.

"That weekend you want to go to the Hamptons is the weekend I was supposed to get married. Before I cancelled the venue and gave back the ring, that was the weekend. I haven't thought about it in a while but then at dinner your sister brought up the holiday weekend and I just thought I should mention it."

"His loss," Max replies and I fall a little bit more in love with him. "I'm sorry that he hurt you," he adds, "but I'm not sorry that it led you here. To New York. To me. I'm not sure that I would have found you in Iowa." He grins when he adds the part about Iowa and pulls me a little bit closer to him.

"Yeah, me too." I smile in response. And I am. Happy, that is. I can see now how much better of a fit I am with Max than I ever was with Brad. I loved Brad, I thought I was going to marry him and spend the rest of my life with him. But I'm grateful that I didn't. That it didn't get that far. I might have chosen a different way to end it, but looking back I can't say it wasn't for the best that it ended. This thing with Max might be new, but it's easy. It's so much easier between us, like I've known him for years instead of weeks. He's so transparent with me, I never feel like I have to guess what he's thinking or what he really wants.

"So, full disclosure," Max repeats before a random passerby interrupts and asks where the nearest subway entrance is. Max directs them over to the Christopher Street Station and then the light changes and we cross the street. Then we run into the drugstore and I realize he never finished his sentence.

"Did you want to tell me something?" I ask as we exit the store.

"Yeah, we were dangerously close to being out of condoms," he says, holding up the bag.

"No." I roll my eyes in his face. "Before. When we were interrupted? Also, I'm on the pill by the way."

"Okay, whoa," he says, holding up his hands. "There's no 'by the way' about that statement, Lauren. Because if that was a green light to fuck you bare then that was the focal point of everything you just said. That's all I heard anyway. I've already blacked out on the rest." He turns me in the direction of his apartment with a firm hand on my back and nudges me to walk, his hand remaining in place as we go lest I might slow my steps and need to be prodded. "Should we get a cab?"

"Your apartment is literally around the corner," I say, pointing. "It's a tenth of a mile and with the one-way streets it would take longer to cab than walk, and why am I even entertaining this question with a response?" But I laugh because I know he's half serious and I love that about him.

"Shit, Lauren." He shakes his head like something's just occurred to him.

"What?"

"It's not even my birthday," he says softly. Then he winks and he's so freaking cute I'm about two seconds from handing him my panties on the sidewalk.

And then I'm not.

We should have turned left when we exited Rite Aid. We should have turned left and taken Tenth to Bleecker. Fuck it all to hell, why didn't we turn left?

Ten

We turned right.

We turned right to take Charles to Bleecker.

We turned right, which took us past the Irish pub on the corner. And in *only in New York* fashion we bumped smack into my ex-fiancé, Brad. Eight million people in New York, one point six million people in Manhattan alone and who do we bump into? The last guy I'm interested in seeing.

I haven't seen him in the ten months since we broke up, not once. I always imagined I'd bump into him again, but in Iowa. We'd both be home for the holidays and run into each other at the Hy-Vee while picking up a last-minute ingredient for Christmas dinner. Or maybe at the airport, waiting for a flight back to New York. But in Manhattan, I assumed I was safe from any awkward encounters.

I see him before he sees me. He's directly in front of me but he's not facing my direction. He's looking behind him, reaching for someone's hand. A woman. She's pretty, I find myself noticing in a detached way. I feel flushed, the way you do when you're surprised by something, because I'm surprised to see him. But I'm not sure I feel anything else. I wait, expecting to feel a bite of pain or hurt, but it's not there. I find myself hoping he's grown up, if not for his own sake then for hers. Whoever she is.

Brad turns and recognition crosses his face—but he's not looking at me. He's looking at Max. "Hey, man," he's calling out a second before my brain registers what's happening. Before I realize they know each other. A heartbeat before I observe something in Max's expression that makes me realize that not only does he know Brad, he knows exactly who Brad is to me. That this is *the* Brad. This all happens in a moment but it feels like slow motion, my brain a step behind. It's not a New York minute, that's for sure. It's more of a microwave minute. You know? How a minute spent waiting for something to cook in the microwave feels like five? Sorta like that.

Then Brad's gaze moves from Max to me, to Max's hand around my shoulder, and a flash of surprise crosses his face at seeing us together.

"Hey, Lauren," Brad says, glancing between us again. "It's good to see you. I didn't realize you two knew each other."

I'm not sure what to say to that because I wasn't aware of this connection until just now, but before I need to respond he's introducing the woman by his side. He introduces her as his girlfriend and after a pause he mentions that they met a few months ago. I suppose this is for my benefit, some kindness he's bestowing on me so that I don't wonder if it's her underwear I found in the apartment I shared with him. I realize as he says it that I wasn't wondering. That it feels like forever ago. That I simply don't care.

Besides, I'm too busy wondering how my ex knows my current boyfriend. I'll be damned if I'm going to ask right now though.

Brad asks about my job and how I'm doing. If I've gotten my own place yet or if I'm still at the bunk bed apartment. I give him the generic answers you give to someone you don't know well enough to elaborate with.

"Babe," the girlfriend says with a slight tug to Brad's arm. I've already forgotten her name. She's pretty. Docile, would be my brief impression. "We're going to be late for the movie," she tells him.

He nods at her and tells me it was good to see me. To take care. He tells Max he'll see him on Monday. So that answers that. They work together.

I'm silent as I watch them walk away, but I slide out from under Max's arm. When they've crossed Charles I turn and look at him.

"I was going to tell you," he starts. Which is never a good way to start a conversation with a woman. How do men not know this? All men past the age of eighteen should know this. They should share this information with each other, pass it along while they do their bro hugs or add it to condom reviews they post online. Write it on bathroom walls if that's what it takes to get the message out.

"What the fuck, Max?"

"On a scale of one to breaking up with me, how mad are you?"

"I'm twenty-three, Max, not thirteen. We're going to have a conversation about this, not pick out a dramatic breakup song."

"Okay." He nods slowly, some of the tension leaving his forehead.

"So you and Brad work together?"

"Sorta," he says and when I raise an eyebrow he adds, "Technically, I'm his boss."

"For fuck's sake," I say, throwing up my hands as I

start walking towards his apartment. "So when exactly did you realize that?" I stop walking and look at him. "Did you always know? Because Brad"—I point in the direction he just walked—"clearly didn't know."

"No. I didn't always know. The first night," he says. "While we were eating takeout you said something about an ex in finance, which could have been one of ten thousand guys in this city. But then you mentioned being from Iowa and a few other things and it all fell into place."

"Why wouldn't you just tell me that?" I'm incredulous.

"Because you'd made some comments about the kind of guys Brad associated with and I didn't want you to write me off before you gave me a chance. I thought you'd walk out the door if I told you then. Also, to be fair, you were half naked at the time and I might not have been thinking rationally."

"You're so stupid."

"Agreed."

"Okay." I sigh. We've reached his apartment and we pause in front of the door and stare at each other. "Let's go fuck this out."

"Seriously?"

"Yes."

"You really are too good to me."

"Agreed. Now unlock the door."

***

We're both laughing when he unlocks the door and kicks it shut behind us, pausing only long enough to flip the deadbolt before he's jogging up the stairs behind me. It's not our first date, we're civilized fuckers now. Which basically means anywhere except the staircase. Because have you ever on a staircase? His stairs are wood, which doesn't help. Not that carpet would help much because rug burns are no joke, especially in the summer when you want to wear a knee-length dress to work the next day.

"I've got something for you," he says when we reach the top of the stairs. "I've been waiting all night to give it to you."

"I know, I've been waiting all night to get it," I agree with a glance at his pants.

"Clearly I'm the romantic in this relationship, you little pervert," he says with a shake of his head as he drops my weekend bag on his dining room table. A table that seats six that we've never eaten at. I love the wide-open lofty feel of his place. It's relaxing and makes me feel like I can unwind. Like I can spread out in the middle of a city that's overcrowded, when I'm normally forced to squeeze myself in.

"Table sex?" I ask, because we've never done that.

"No," he retorts with a snort then pauses. "Well, maybe. Let's not discount that. But first," he says, handing me a small box that must have been waiting on the dining table.

I take it from him and examine it in my hands. It's about the size of a pack of gum, but thicker. It's cardboard with a twine string wrapped around it and fastened under a little disk attached to the top. It's not fancy—urban hip, maybe. I flick my eyes up to his and then back to the box in my hands.

"It's not my birthday either," I point out.

"Open it," he urges.

I unwrap the twine and the cardboard unfolds to reveal another cardboard box, this one with corrugated edges and a top flap that slides out to open. I run my fingers over the edges for a second, enjoying the way the material feels under my fingertips and enjoying the sweet moment.

Then I slide the top flap open and look inside, confused for a moment about what I'm looking at. It's a fortune, like from a fortune cookie. But it's inside of a small glass-fronted box. "Is this—" I begin to ask as I pull it from the box and the chain dangles free. "It's a necklace," I coo. It's gorgeous, the slimmest rose-gold box dangling from a matching chain. I pull it closer to read what's written on the paper. It is a fortune—I was right about that. It says, *Don't be afraid to smile. You never know who's falling in love with it.*

"Max." I grin. "I love it." I slide it over my head, the chain long enough to allow me to put it on without unclasping it. Once it's on I finger the locket between my fingers and look up at Max with a smile so big I bite my lip to try to contain it. "Thank you."

"You're welcome."

"Is this the fortune you wouldn't read to me that night? On our first date?"

He nods.

"Because you already loved my smile? Even then?"

"Because I already knew I could love you, even then."

"You did?" I ask.

"I do," he corrects. "Love you."

"I didn't," I say with an almost imperceptible shake of my head. "I didn't know it yet then. But I do now. Well, I knew a while ago. I think technically you got to me while we were eating food from a street vendor. You were—" I don't get to finish that thought because sex is apparently back on the table. Literally. My ass is on the table and my dress is being lifted over my head.

"No," Max says, pulling away from me. His lips were just on mine and I lean forward as he pulls back as if I can drag him back to my lips by sheer force of will.

"No?" He's such a fucking tease, this guy.

"Not on the table," he says and slides me off the edge, my legs wrapping around his hips as he does. "Not on the table right now," he adds. "I'm not conceding the table as a viable surface for any future fuckery. But now, bed."

"How caveman of you," I tell him, tugging at his earlobe with my teeth and doing my best to gyrate myself against him, to get the friction I desperately want on my clit. "I like it."

"Of course you do." He sets me on my feet at the foot of the stairs and slaps my ass. "Go up. Take off your bra and panties and wait for me on the bed."

"Oh, we're doing a bossy thing too. Me really likey."

"Go." He shakes his head at me and laughs.

Upstairs I slide my underthings off and drop them on a chair in his bedroom. Then I take the necklace off and examine it again before I place it on his dresser. I don't want the chain to tangle, and if it stays on it's going to end up wrapped up in my hair. I notice there's a tiny hinge on the box and clasp that opens the glass lid, so I can switch out the fortune if I want. I can't imagine wanting to though, it's perfect just as it is. I run my fingers along the glass window and smile, remembering our first night together. Remembering the first time we met when he said something about enjoying my laugh. That he liked my smile.

"Why aren't you in bed?" Max enters the room, pulling his shirt off and giving me a pointed look. "Your instructions were naked and in bed. You are naked, which I appreciate, but you're not in bed, which I don't." He unbuckles his belt, his movements unhurried, his fingers nimble as the belt falls open and he unzips his pants. Flicking his eyes back to mine, he grins, that damn dimple

JANA ASTON

of his making me wetter than I already am. "Wait, are you trying to ask me for some kinky spanking shit? Where you deliberately don't follow instructions and then I pretend to be cross with you and bend you over my knee? Because I'm on page eighty of this month's book club pick and I haven't come across any spanking scenes yet so I'm not sure what we're doing here." He grins when he says it, and his tone is teasing so I'm not taking him seriously.

"No." I shake my head with a laugh. "I wasn't."

"Good, because that shit never turns out as hot as you think it's going to. It looks good in movies but here, without the correct lighting and someone filming it, it's just kinda awkward." He shoves his pants over his hips, his cock heavy, the small talk doing nothing to dull his erection. "But hey, if it's your sexual fantasy I'm willing to oblige you."

"It's not. I mean, let's not take it off the table"—I wink at him—"but not right now."

"Okay, I'll practice. Just so I'm prepared if you change your mind."

"Wait, how in the hell are you going to practice spanking?"

"Really?" He raises a brow, his expression amused. "Did you really just ask me that? I was a teenage boy once."

"Stop." I laugh. "How are you going to practice spanking me?"

"I don't know." He shrugs. "A pillow?"

"I don't think so."

"What? It could work." He grabs a pillow from the bed and gives it a thwack. It makes the same sound as fluffing a pillow, which is ridiculous. I frown and shake my head at him. "That's a good girl, take it," he says, giving the pillow another whack as he drops onto the bed.

Shit. "Okay, that good girl thing was hot," I admit, my eyes darting away and then back again. He looks interested in this revelation but I hold up a hand as I set the necklace down and walk towards him. "Can I ask you something?" I ask, bending one knee onto the bed.

"Of course."

"That night we met," I start and I see the recognition flash across his face. He knows where I'm going with this. "When I was blogging at Starbucks. You just flirted with me and left. What if you'd never seen me again?"

"Lauren." He smiles and holds his hand out to me until I lean forward and crawl over him, resting my head on his chest. "My gym is around the corner from that Starbucks. I'd seen you in there at least half a dozen times."

"You had?" I ask, surprised. "Why'd you wait so long to talk to me?"

"I didn't think you were ready."

"You didn't?" I question. But he's right, I wasn't.

"That night was the first time you ever looked up. The first time you ever caught me staring at you."

"That's not creepy," I joke while tapping his chest with my fingers.

"I knew I'd see you there again. And I figured eventually I'd wear you down."

"Still a little creepy," I say, holding my finger and thumb apart an inch.

"But then I bumped into you the next day on the subway. Wearing a wedding dress and examining the Times Square mosaic like it was your job."

"I really do love those mosaics," I mumble.

"Giving me shit about threesomes and coming up

with every excuse you could think of not to go out with me."

"Oh, yeah, the threesomes." I laugh. "I was convinced you were going to ask me to some kind of kinky sex party."

"You wish." He flips us over so he's on top and tugs a nipple between his teeth. "But I'm not sharing you. You're mine."

"I like being yours," I tell him, lacing my fingers into his hair.

"So we're good?" he asks.

"So good," I agree. "Now stop messing around and give it to me."

"Give it to you? I don't think you're a good girl after all. I think you're a bad girl."

"Can't I be both?"

"I like the way your dirty mind works." He winks. "Now why don't you be a good girl and put your hands above your head."

I do. Of course I do.

His cock is heavy against my stomach as he cups my jaw and works his lips down the column of my neck. I love the way it feels when his dick is hard and pressed between us, so close to where I want it. I like the weight of it, the warmth. I shift my legs open and rotate my hips, hoping to appeal directly to his penis in my quest to get what I want.

"Ask nicely," he teases. Oh, I like this game.

"Please?" I ask.

"Try harder," he says, trailing his lips down to my tits. He's not teasing either, he can work me for what feels like forever. Toying with me, kissing every inch of my body. Pressing my tits together and sliding his cock between them, then sliding down to taste me while palming his dick in long slow strokes.

"Please give me your cock," I try.

"All those books you read and that's the best you've got?" He shakes his head and manages a look of disappointment, but his lip pulls into a small smile, giving him away.

"I want to feel you bare inside of me," I tell him, biting my lip. "I want you to fuck me like you own me, Max," I tell him, looking him dead in the eye. "Hold me down and take what you want."

"Jesus," he mutters and flips me over. A second later my thighs are spread wide and he's inside of me. I groan and keep my arms stretched over my head, palms spread against the headboard, my forehead against the pillow while he moves. It's so deep like this and I squeeze myself around his shaft and moan into the pillow. Over and over again he drives into me and when I try to snake a hand down to my clit, he grabs my wrist and bends my arm behind my back. He places his other hand on the back of my neck and squeezes lightly, so lightly, and I might have even more deviant potential than I thought because it only takes me another minute to come like this. The spasms seem like they go on forever, Max letting go of my arm and wrist and wrapping his hands around my waist as he continues to pump into me until he follows me over the edge.

"Remind me never to challenge you," he says after, when he's wrapped around me, my back to his front, his mouth to my ear. "You're going to kill me."

"It'd be a hell of a way to go though."

"Was that makeup sex? We didn't even have a real fight. Wow."

"Rational conversation," I remind him sleepily.

"So we got to skip the fight and go right to the makeup sex," he muses. "Fuck, I'm the luckiest man alive."

"Don't press your luck. We can still have a fight if you're that into it."

"No, I'm good."

"Thought so."

"I'm getting a sign made though. For over the bed."

"What?" I ask, turning my head to look at him.

"You know how people hang motivational shit over their bed like *Always Kiss Me Goodnight?*"

"Yeah."

"Ours will say, *Skip the fight. Go right to the make-up sex.*"

"You really are the romantic in this relationship."

"That's why you love me."

"It is," I agree and then snuggle back into his arms and close my eyes, totally content with the fairy tale I found right in the middle of my ordinary life.

Epilogue

"So we're really doing this?" He grins at me, those dimples no less effective on me than they were the first time I saw them four months ago.

"We're really doing this," I agree, pausing to look at him. "Unless you don't want to?"

"Of course I want to, crazy girl. As long as this is what you want. I want you to have the perfect day. Fly your family in, go to Iowa, Vegas, I don't care as long as you're happy."

"Honestly, Max, I just want you." I gather the skirt of my dress in my hands so it won't drag on the sidewalk. "And this dress," I add with a grin. "The dress is really the only wedding detail I care about. I don't need a perfect Pinterest wedding. Just the perfect guy, the perfect dress and—"

"And city hall," Max finishes.

"And city hall," I confirm. "Let's do this."

"You're sure you don't want me to call a car service?" he asks as we step onto the sidewalk outside his—our— apartment.

"No way, Subway or bust," I tell him.

Unofficially we've been living together since summer. In September I made it official and gave up my bunk bed spot to another girl.

In October Max proposed. A two-carat cushion-cut diamond in a halo setting, which I care about because he picked it out himself, but I'd have said yes to a ring made with a gum wrapper. The part I love about it the most is what's engraved inside the band: *Your smile changed my life.*

Today I'll slide a ring onto Max's finger with an engraving of my own. *Your love changed mine.*

End of Book Notes

Thank you for reading Times Square! I hope you enjoyed Max & Lauren's story.

Join my reader group on Facebook: bit.ly/2eXkdpA

Shameless plea for you to join my newsletter (bit.ly/2edgQbm) where you'll always be notified of new releases, special offers, signing events & any other fun things I can come up with!

Thank you, thank you, thank you for reading.
xo, Jana

Facebook: Jana Aston
Twitter: @janaaston
Website: Janaaston.com
Instagram: SteveCatnip

Also by Jana Aston

The Wrong series

Wrong
Right
Fling
Trust

About Jana

Jana Aston likes cats, big coffee cups and books about billionaires who deflower virgins. She wrote her debut novel while fielding customer service calls about electrical bills, and she's ever grateful for the fictional gynecologist in Wrong that readers embraced so much she was able to make working in her pajamas a reality.

Jana's work has appeared on the NYT, WSJ and USA Today bestsellers lists, some multiple times. She likes multiples.